Written by Kim Gosselin

Illustrated by Thom Buttner

JayJo Books

Special Books for Special Kids®

Smoking STINKS!!
© 1998 by Kim Gosselin
Edited by Barbara Mitchell
Design by Carol Stanton

Published by
JayJo Books
Publishing *Special Books for Special Kids*®

JayJo Books is a publisher of books to help teachers, parents, and children cope with chronic illnesses, special needs, and health education in classroom, family, and social settings.

Library of Congress Control Number 97-71950
ISBN 10: 1-891383-20-5
ISBN 13: 978-1-891383-20-5
Second Edition
First book in our *Substance Free Kids*® series

For all information, including
Premium and Special Sales, contact:
JayJo Books
A Brand of The Guidance Group
www.guidance-group.com

Here's What Professionals Are Saying About Smoking STINKS!!

An Excellent Resource!!

*"**Smoking STINKS!!** is A VITAL TOOL in teaching our children the dangers of tobacco use. I know about those dangers firsthand as I watched my father and oldest brother die from cigarette-caused diseases. This terrific book should be in every child's library and in every school!"*

— PATRICK REYNOLDS, GRANDSON OF R.J. REYNOLDS
President, The Foundation for a Smokefree America
Beverly Hills, California

Expertly Done and Long Overdue!

*"As we continue to learn more about the addictive cycle of cigarette smoking, it is vital that we teach our children the importance of staying tobacco free. **Smoking STINKS!!** is a fun way for kids to learn about the dangers of tobacco use without the appearance of 'teaching.' Studies clearly indicate that smoking is a pediatric disease—one which must be stopped in adolescence in order to truly impact the number of Americans who die prematurely each year as a result of smoking. The American Cancer Society hopes that the lessons in this new 'Substance Free Kids' book will further contribute to nationwide efforts to protect our children from becoming addicted to tobacco."*

— ELIZABETH BRIDGERS
Director, National Communications
American Cancer Society

A Powerful Message!

*"**Smoking STINKS!!** sends a powerful message to children that nicotine is a drug and that smoking causes death and disease. This book also stresses that there is no safe tobacco. Cigarette smoking in children is in epidemic proportions, and as these children become addicted to tobacco before the age of 20, a third of them will die from this addiction. **Smoking STINKS!!** is an excellent, helpful, and educational tool for all young children."*

— LINDA B. FORD, M.D.
Past President, American Lung Association
The Asthma and Allergy Center
Papillion, Nebraska

Heartwarming and Educational!!

*"Cigarette smoking is the single most important risk factor for lung and heart disease. Keeping children from starting to smoke is the most important thing that society can do to improve everyone's health. **Smoking STINKS!!** presents important information clearly and in a way that children can easily understand. Kim Gosselin's book is an excellent contribution to education of all children about this very important health concern."*

— ROBERT C. STRUNK, M.D.
Director, Division of Allergy and Pulmonary Medicine
Washington University School of Medicine
Saint Louis, Missouri

Well Done!! A "Must Have"!!

*"Cigarette smoking is an important child health concern. **Smoking STINKS!!** is a wonderfully crafted illustration of how significant this issue is for children with allergies and asthma. Congratulations to Kim Gosselin on creating another remarkable work of art, which educates children on the need for avoiding cigarette smoke, while imparting the critical message to never begin smoking. This first book in the 'Substance Free Kids' series gives children and families courage and support to understand and talk about difficult issues."*

— PHILLIP E. KORENBLAT, M.D.
Professor of Clinical Medicine
Washington University School of Medicine
Medical Director of The Asthma Center
Director of Clinical Research
Barnes-Jewish West County Hospital
Saint Louis, Missouri

A True Winner!!

*"Cigarette smoking is harmful to the smoker and to those around them. Kim Gosselin has produced a wonderful educational book to assist children in learning about this health problem. As in her other well-illustrated books, she presents the information in a manner that children can understand. The message is clear: '**Smoking STINKS!!**'"*

— GARY S. RACHELEFSKY, M.D.
Clinical Professor, Pediatrics
University of California at Los Angeles
Director, Allergy Research Foundation, Inc.

Great Education for Kids!

Smoking STINKS!! *gets the message about the harmful and unpleasant effects of smoking across in a way that is clearly portrayed and appealing to children and students. Good educational practice relates learning to students' life experiences. Kim Gosselin's book does so in a convincing and eminently appealing fashion. If we can ingrain the message in students' minds during elementary and middle school, they will be much better equipped to resist the temptation to smoke later in life."*

— MICHAEL CERUTTI, PRINCIPAL
Wren Hollow Elementary School

Acknowledgments

I wish to thank the American Lung Association and the American Cancer Society for their support of my work which is dedicated to the enjoyment and education of all children, particularly those living with chronic conditions.

*I also wish to extend my sincere appreciation to the many physicians and health professionals who took time out of their extremely busy schedules to review **Smoking STINKS!!***

— Kim Gosselin

About the Author

__Kim Gosselin__ began her writing career with a heartfelt desire and determination to educate the classmates of children with special needs and/or chronic conditions. An author of 15 books, Kim is also an avid supporter of the American Lung Association, American Cancer Society, the Epilepsy Foundation of America, American Diabetes Association, Juvenile Diabetes Research Foundation, and CHADD. Kim is extremely committed to bringing the young reader quality health education, while raising important funds for medical research. A recipient of the Environmental Protection Agency Asthma Education Award, the Teachers' Choice Award, and the National American Lung Association Presidential Award, Kim is a member of the Authors Guild and the Society of Children's Book Writers and Illustrators.

A Note from the Author

As a child I was blessed with three loving grandfathers. The memories of my time spent with them are dear to my heart, and I shall treasure them always.

Grandpa "K" delighted in taking me to my first amusement park where I rode the carousel in awe. Grandpa "G" squeezed me tight with loving "bear hugs" and slipped me a dollar whenever he came visiting. "Little" Grandpa lived with me, and was a treasured part of the family (all seventy pounds of him). As I grew older, he convincingly praised my canned spaghetti dinners, and played soulful songs on his harmonica before climbing into bed each night.

Grandpa "K" smoked cigars and tobacco in a pipe. He died from lung cancer.

Grandpa "G" smoked cigarettes. He died from smoking-related heart disease.

"Little" Grandpa chewed tobacco and smoked cigarettes. He passed away from lung cancer and emphysema.

Smoking STINKS.

Dedicated in loving memory to
Grandpa K., Grandpa G., and Little Grandpa
and to Mother, with all my love.

The bell rang just as Maddie shoved her books into her cubbie and plopped down in her seat. Her friend Alex read the day's announcements. Maddie didn't seem to hear a word.

Mr. Jenkins handed out the class's special assignment reminder. Their health reports were due by Friday. Maddie hadn't even started! She was too worried about her Grandpa Norman. Grandpa Norman had a bad cough. His cough seemed to be getting worse lately. The awful hacking noise coming from Grandpa Norman's bedroom woke Maddie up nearly every night now.

On top of everything else, Maddie's allergies were bugging her again. Grandpa Norman's cigarette smoking always seemed to make her allergies worse! Maddie grabbed a tissue from the space under her desk and wiped her dribbling nose. **"SMOKING STINKS!!"** she shouted aloud.

Maddie looked up sheepishly.
Fifty-two enormous round eyes,
in various shades of brown, blue, and green,
stared straight through her!

"Do you have something you'd like to share with the class, MISS MADELINE?" Mr. Jenkins asked, as only HE could.

"I'm sorry," Maddie apologized, her face turning redder than her strawberry blond hair.

"I thought you mentioned something about smoking?" Mr. Jenkins inquired. "Would you care to share the topic of your health report with the class NOW?"

"Health report?" Maddie's heart pounded fiercely. "Oh, yeah!" she bounced back. "My health report's going to be um.... about smoking."

"Great topic!" said Mr. Jenkins. "I'm sure the whole class would agree with you, that smoking, indeed, STINKS!"

The giggles subsided as Maddie sank deeper and deeper into her chair. She couldn't wait until the school day was over; and yet, it had only just begun.

4TH GRADE ART

LISA

Later, Maddie tried to concentrate on her new spelling words. She doodled clouds of smoke in the margins of her notebook paper, and wrapped a loose curl around her forefinger. Finally, it was time for lunch. Maddie grabbed her lunch bag and headed towards the cafeteria. Her friend, Alex, caught up with her, just as the rest of the class rounded the hall corner.

"Hey, Maddie! My health report's on smoking too," he announced.

"Let's ask Mr. Jenkins if we can work together."

"Are you sure you wouldn't be too embarrassed?" she asked, accusingly.

"Naw," he replied, tearing into his bag of chips.

"Besides, smoking does STINK....in more ways than one."

"What do you mean?" she asked, sitting down next to him.

"Well, my mom smokes too," Alex said, munching on a potato chip. "Our whole house stinks like a chimney. Plus, I've got asthma. Breathing in somebody else's smoke usually makes it even worse!"

"Yeah, it bothers my allergies too," Maddie said. "SMOKING STINKS!!" she said again, while taking a big bite out of the apple from her lunch bag.

After lunch, Maddie and Alex talked to Mr. Jenkins about working together on their health report. Mr. Jenkins thought it was a great idea! He even suggested they find a guest speaker to come in and talk to the class with them.

That night, Alex and Maddie worked on their health report at Grandpa Norman and Maddie's kitchen table. They asked Grandpa Norman a million questions about smoking. Maddie and Alex took turns scribbling down notes in their spiral binders while listening to Grandpa Norman speak.

"Why did you ever start smoking?" asked Alex. "Because I thought it was cool," he answered, disgusted with his dirty ashtray sitting on the table. "I was about fifteen at the time. All my friends were smoking, and I just wanted to be like them."

"Why don't you quit?" asked Maddie, simply.

"Oh, Maddie," Grandpa said, "I've tried so many times. You see, it's not so easy to quit. Smoking is an addiction because tobacco has nicotine in it."

Maddie gulped. "What's NICOTINE?"

Grandpa Norman stared at Maddie and Alex hard. He looked straight into their eyes, hesitating only to stop and catch his breath. "Nicotine is poison!" he said, lightly pounding his fist on the kitchen table. "It's a very powerful DRUG!!"

"Wow," gasped Alex. "A drug! No wonder my mom said smoking cigarettes was a lot like taking drugs. She told me her brain knows smoking's bad for her, but her body feels like she really NEEDS it."

"That's exactly right!" Grandpa Norman said, struggling to get up and out of his chair. "An addiction means that it's hard to stop. And it doesn't matter if you smoke cigars, a pipe, cigarettes, or use chewing or 'spit' tobacco— the addiction is the same. The smartest thing you kids can do is to NEVER start!!"

Maddie and Alex
sat glued to their seats.
Neither one of them said a word.
They thought about the many times they
had seen some of the older kids hanging around the
high school. A lot of them smoked cigarettes or chewed tobacco
like Grandpa Norman mentioned. Maddie especially hated it when they
spit their gross tobacco juice out on the sidewalk!

Grandpa Norman went on to tell Maddie and Alex about the many different diseases smoking could cause. He rattled off words Maddie and Alex could hardly even say. Words like BRONCHITIS and EMPHYSEMA. And then, of course, he reminded them about things they already knew about. Things like HEART DISEASE and CANCER.

Maddie had heard the word EMPHYSEMA before. She heard Grandpa Norman talking to Doctor Parkin about it on the phone. She wondered if emphysema was what made Grandpa Norman cough so much. Did emphysema make it hard for him to even breathe?

Later, after Alex had gone home, Grandpa Norman tucked Maddie into bed. She saw the ugly brown stains on his fingers from the tobacco in his cigarettes, and smelled the smoke in his favorite flannel nightshirt. Maddie understood things better now. She understood that Grandpa Norman was probably addicted to nicotine. Even so, she loved him with all her heart!

Maddie asked Grandpa Norman if he would be a guest speaker for her health report on Friday. He said he'd be glad to, especially if he could help stop kids from making some of the same mistakes that he had! He even promised to ask Doctor Parkin to come along. Dr. Parkin could be a guest speaker too!

The rest of the week, Maddie and Alex worked hard at school on their health report. Doctor Parkin let them borrow a giant poster. It showed a picture of two lungs. One of them was healthy and pink (the way lungs should be). But the other lung was brown and sick-looking (from smoking). "Smoking STINKS!!" thought Maddie and Alex, as they hung the poster up on the classroom wall.

Finally it was Friday! Maddie and Alex shared their health report on smoking with Mr. Jenkins and the whole class. Doctor Parkin stood in the front of the room and told the kids how smoking caused many, many people to get very sick. "A lot of people get sick and even die EVERY DAY from smoking-related diseases," Dr. Parkin said, sadly.

Next, Dr. Parkin talked about "passive" or "secondhand" smoke (breathing in the smoke of someone's burning cigar or cigarette). He said secondhand smoke was bad for ANYBODY to breathe. But it could be much worse for kids who were living with allergies or asthma. Gertie, in the third row, raised her right hand.

"I have asthma," she said. "You mean, if I breathe in somebody else's smoke, my asthma might get worse?" "That's possible," answered Dr. Parkin, while Alex and Maddie nodded in agreement. "Smoke of any kind can help trigger an asthma episode."

"What about 'spit' tobacco?" asked the tall skinny kid with glasses. "I see a lot of baseball players using it, so it must be safe, right?"

"WRONG!" answered Dr. Parkin, firmly. "Chewing or 'spit' tobacco can lead to many of the same problems other tobacco causes, or even start new ones! Just remember kids, there is NO SAFE TOBACCO!!!"

Next it was Grandpa Norman's turn to speak.

First, he did something the kids thought was pretty weird.

Grandpa Norman passed around his favorite flannel

night shirt for all of them to SMELL!

"GROSS!!" said Gertie, taking in a big whiff.

"Smoking STINKS!!!"

Grandpa Norman nodded, and went on to tell the kids about his experiences with smoking. "When I was a teenager," he said, "nobody seemed to know how bad smoking was. Now, we all know differently!"

"There's **NOTHING** good about smoking," Grandpa Norman said, sitting down to catch his breath.

"Have you ever tried to quit?" asked another girl in the back of the room.

"I'm ALWAYS trying to quit," he said. "Nobody WANTS to get sick," Grandpa Norman added, pointing to Dr. Parkin's lung poster. "Nobody wants to wake up coughing every night. And, believe me, it's real scary when you don't know if you'll be able to catch another breath or not!"

Grandpa Norman told the class that sometimes (with a lot of help from their doctor, family and friends), people WERE able to quit smoking.

"It takes a lot of courage, and support," Grandpa Norman said, glancing at Dr. Parkin and Maddie.

"As of today, I've smoked my last cigarette!"

"Smoking's not as awesome as some of those older kids think!" Alex shouted defiantly. "Smoking STINKS!!" blurted out Maddie, in her loudest, biggest voice ever! This time, nobody giggled. Instead, the whole class stood up and cheered.

"Smoking STINKS!!"

...they all yelled together.... even Mr. Jenkins!

The End

Additional Resources

The following professional organizations may help provide additional education and support.

AMERICAN LUNG ASSOCIATION
1740 Broadway
New York, NY 10019
800.LUNG.USA
www.lungusa.org

AMERICAN CANCER SOCIETY
1599 Clifton Road NE
Atlanta, GA 30329
800.ACS.2345
www.cancer.org

AMERICAN HEART ASSOCIATION
7272 Greenville Avenue
Dallas, TX 75231
800.AHA.USA1
www.americanheart.org

AMERICAN ACADEMY OF PEDIATRICS
141 NW Point Boulevard
Elk Grove Village, IL 60007
847.434.4000
www.aap.org

AMERICAN ACADEMY OF ALLERGY, ASTHMA AND IMMUNOLOGY
611 East Wells Street
Milwaukee, WI 53202
800.822.2762
www.aaaai.org

CAMPAIGN FOR TOBACCO-FREE KIDS
1400 Eye Street
Suite 1200
Washington, DC 20005
202.296.5469
800.284.KIDS
www.tobaccofreekids.org

THE FOUNDATION FOR A SMOKEFREE AMERICA
PO Box 492028
Los Angeles, CA 90049-8028
310.471.4270
www.tobaccofree.org

Patrick Reynolds, grandson of tobacco company founder R.J. Reynolds, is a nationally known tobacco-free advocate. Call The Foundation for a Smokefree America or visit their website to find out how you can arrange for Mr. Reynolds to bring the smoke-free message to students in your community.

To order additional copies of **Smoking STINKS!!** or inquire about our quantity discounts for schools, hospitals, and affiliated organizations, contact us at 1-800-999-6884.

From our *Special Kids in School®* series

Taking A.D.D. to School	Taking Diabetes to School
Taking Arthritis to School	Taking Down Syndrome to School
Taking Asthma to School	Taking Dyslexia to School
Taking Autism to School	Taking Food Allergies to School
Taking Cancer to School	Taking Hearing Impairment to School
Taking Cerebral Palsy to School	Taking Seizure Disorders to School
Taking Cystic Fibrosis to School	Taking Speech Disorders to School
Taking Depression to School	Taking Tourette Syndrome to School

...and others coming soon!

From our *Healthy Habits for Kids®* series
There's a Louse in My House
A Fun Story about Kids and Head Lice

From our *Special Family and Friends™* series
Allie Learns About Alzheimer's Disease
A Family Story about Love, Patience, and Acceptance

Patrick Learns About Parkinson's Disease
A Story of a Special Bond Between Friends
...and others coming soon!

Other books available now!
SPORTSercise!
A "School" Story about Exercise-Induced Asthma

ZooAllergy
A Fun Story about Allergy and Asthma Triggers

Rufus Comes Home
Rufus the Bear with Diabetes™
A Story about Diagnosis and Acceptance

The ABC's of Asthma
An Asthma Alphabet Book for Kids of All Ages

Trick or Treat for Diabetes
A Halloween Story for Kids Living with Diabetes